UP CLOSE

CORAL

A CLOSE-UP PHOTOGRAPHIC LOOK INSIDE YOUR WORLD

Written by Heidi Fiedler

This library edition published in 2017 by Walter Foster Jr.,
an imprint of The Quarto Group
6 Orchard Road, Suite 100
Lake Forest, CA 92630

Project Editor: Heidi Fiedler
Written by Heidi Fiedler
Photographs on pages 12, 14, 26, and 32 by Henry Jager.
All other images © Shutterstock.

Distributed in the United States and Canada by
Lerner Publisher Services
241 First Avenue North
Minneapolis, MN 55401 U.S.A.
www.lernerbooks.com

First Library Edition

Library of Congress Cataloging-in-Publication Data

Names: Fiedler, Heidi, author.
Title: Coral : a close-up photographic look inside your world / written by Heidi Fiedler.
Description: First library edition. | Lake Forest, CA : Walter Foster Publishing, 2017. | Audience: Ages 8+. | Includes bibliographical references and index.
Identifiers: LCCN 2017011689 | ISBN 9781942875352 (hardcover : alk. paper)
Subjects: LCSH: Corals--Juvenile literature. | Shells--Juvenile literature. | Photography, Close-up--Juvenile literature.
Classification: LCC QL377.C5 F477 2017 | DDC 593.6--dc23
LC record available at https://lccn.loc.gov/2017011689

Printed in USA
9 8 7 6 5 4 3 2 1

Are You Ready for Your Close-up?

Can you feel your brain tickling? That's the magic of looking at something way UP CLOSE. It transforms the ordinary into something new and strange and inspires everyone from hi-tech shutterbugs and supersmart scientists to look again. So let's turn the ZOOM up to eleven and discover a whole new way of seeing the world.

Carnation coral

How Eye See the World

"Whatcha lookin' at?" That's the question people have been asking each other for thousands of years. The first humans observed interesting—and important—things like woolly mammoths, lightning, and each other. Early artists moved on to painting and drawing what they saw. Finally, in 1862, photography allowed people to capture what they saw in new and amazing ways.

Today, photographs are everywhere. Cereal boxes, bulletin boards, and T-shirts are all home to photos. A simple image search online can produce cootchie-cootchie-coo images of bright-eyed babies or stark, white, snowy landscapes. Photographers capture everything from moments of joy and pain to the wonders that exist in the cracks and hidden layers of our busy world. They focus their attention on a huge range of subjects, and the images they produce reveal how everyone sees the world in their own unique way.

The History of Photography

Black-and-White Photography

1826
Nicéphore Niépce creates the first photograph. It takes 8 hours.

1859
Photography goes panoramic.

1839
Daguerreotypes capture rough images on pieces of metal.

1877
Eadweard Muybridge invents a way to shoot objects—such as horses—in motion.

Color Photography

1888
Kodak™ produces the first mass-produced camera.

1912
The 35mm camera takes center stage.

1930
Flash bulbs help photographers capture images in low light.

1935
New techniques make color photography shine.

1939
An electron microscope reveals what a virus looks like.

1946
Zoomar produces the zoom lens.

Digital Photography

1976
Canon® produces the first camera with a microprocessor.

"Photography...has little to do with the things you see and everything to do with the way you see them."
—Elliott Erwitt

1992
The first JPEG is produced.

2015
Instagram is home to more than 20 billion images.

Extreme Close-up!

Photography has been helping people express how they see the world for nearly 200 years, and in that time, things have gone way beyond taking a simple shot of a horse or a sunset. Today, photographers are pushing the limits of technology.

Macro photographers use large lenses to get WAY up close to their subjects. They can magnify an object to more than five times its size, using special lenses that reveal patterns and textures that wow viewers.

Knobby starfish

Micro photography goes even further. It uses a microscope to reveal details humans could never see before. It can make coral look like a glowing planet or a priceless piece of jewelry.

The deep blue oceans of our planet are some of the last places on Earth that have yet to be explored. And photographers are leading the way. Some are scientists, studying colorful corals of the deep. Others simply love being underwater, where life is more colorful and stranger than we could ever imagine. Take a look!

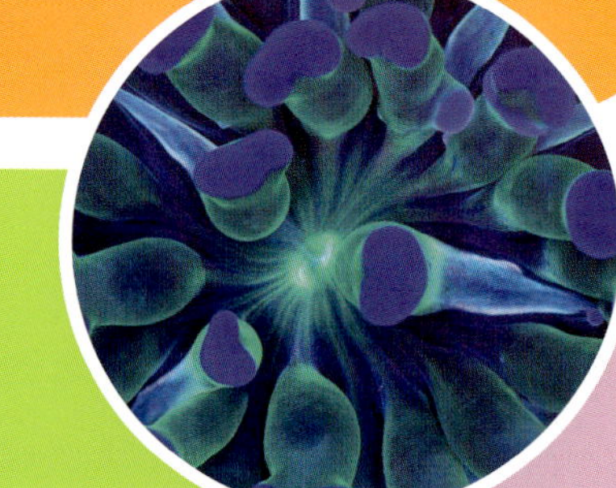

Touch coral

Getting the Shot

Photographers choose where and how they want to work based on what type of images they want to produce.

Clownfish

Out in the Field

Macro photographers can take their giant lenses underwater to capture sea life in its natural environment.

Seashell

In the Studio

Working inside lets photographers have more control over the lighting, the angle of the camera, and their subject.

Seashell

Under the Microscope

A microscope allows photographers to look at their subjects in even more detail.

An Unforgettable Handshake

Introducing the Staghorn Coral

Long alien fingers beckon you closer. But these hands don't belong to little green men. This is a coral—a creature made up of many tiny animals that have grown a hard skeleton. These creatures are so strange; they're almost like aliens living among us. (But they've lived underwater for more than 50 million years!)

Scientific Name: Acroporidae
Size: Branches can grow up to 7 feet
Habitat: Warm ocean water up to 100 feet deep
Diet: Algae living inside the coral produce food for the coral

These coral are known as staghorn or elkhorn because their branches sometimes look like antlers.

The Stories They Could Tell

The largest coral reefs are also the oldest. Acropora corals can grow about 4 inches per year.

My, what BIG lips you have!

Well, HELLO, there!

Presenting Mr. Rock and Roll, also known as Cup Coral! Coral are wildly colorful—and wildly misunderstood—creatures. They may look like flowers, but they're really a type of underwater animal that spends its days eating, swaying in the water, and looking pretty. Oh so pretty!

Scientific Name: Dendrophyllia gracilis
Size: A single polyp can grow up to 12 inches tall
Habitat: Warm waters in the Indian and Pacific oceans
Diet: Small bits of meat

This underwater rock star gets its color from the algae that live inside it.

The Rainforests of the Sea

Nearly 25 percent of all marine creatures depend on coral to survive. Healthy coral are brightly colored. But when these sensitive creatures don't have everything they need to survive, they turn white. Overfishing, pollution, and invasive species all threaten coral.

Coral Close-ups

Coral come in a bonanza of shapes, sizes, and colors! Many coral are made up of tiny, soft polyps, which are translucent animals like jellyfish. Each polyp has a hard base. When a polyp lands on a rock, it divides and multiplies. Then, thousands of polyps connect to one another to form a colony that acts as one structure. The more structures a colony grows, the more places there are for fish and other sea creatures to live. A colony can live for centuries and join together to form reefs large enough to be seen from outer space.

Zoanthid corals

Psychedelic, Baby!

Acan coral

Cup coral

Sunny-side Up

Touch coral

In a Different Light

To our earthly eyes, this coral is throbbing with color. But it depends how you look at it. Out of water, a coral may look brown and dull, because coral evolved to be seen underwater where light is transmitted differently. That same coral can look stunning underwater, because its fluorescent pigments absorb and reflect different colors.

Scientific Name: Favia
Size: Less than an inch in diameter
Habitat: Atlantic and Pacific Oceans
Diet: Krill, brine shrimp, and plankton

The knobby ridges that form the surface of this coral give it the nerdy nickname Brain Coral.

Coral Wars

Corals need their space. If there are other corals in the area, watch out! They'll use their tentacles to capture food—and fend off other corals from feeding in the same area.

The Labyrinth Awaits

A mysterious light twists and turns. You follow it, spiraling deeper and deeper. Is it a portal to another world? As you look closer, you see it's a shell—just like the kind you find on the beach. It's mysterious, glowing in a way that makes you sure that if you could hold it to your ear at just the right angle, you would hear a song of mystical whale calls—which makes it just like every other shell. Mysterious and ordinary all at once.

Scientific Name: Tonna galea
Size: 6 to 10 inches
Habitat: Caribbean Sea and Indo-Pacific waters
Diet: A wide variety of marine animals, including sea cucumbers

The **sulfuric acid** in its **saliva** helps this **snail kill** its **prey.**

Eye Spy

Next time you're at the beach, bring a pocket microscope with you and look at the sand. You'll find each grain looks like its own strange planet.

Spotlight on Seashells

We spend hours at the beach, admiring their beauty, but there's still a lot we don't understand about how marine animals build their shells. What we do know is shells come in all different shapes and sizes. They grow as the creature inside grows. Over time, shells may become cracked or chipped in battle, and their colors may change based on what's in the water. But their main job is to keep clams, snails, and mollusks safe from predators.

Unforgettably Grand

1,000 Shades of White

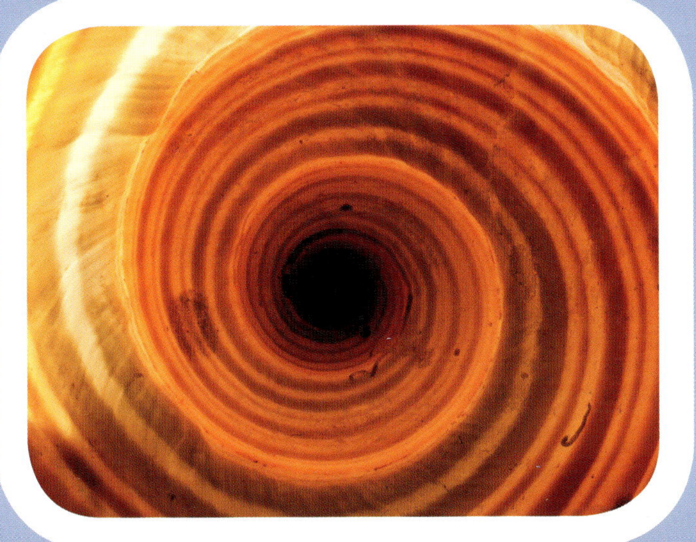

Spiraltastic

Iridescent Wonder

Uniquely Urchin

Wiggly, Jiggly, Painful Little Stinkers

Sea anemones are known for their soft tentacles that float in the water like flower petals blowing in the wind. But they aren't as innocent as they look. Their tentacles are filled with venom. As prey passes by—zap! They strike, stinging their next meal until it's paralyzed and can be eaten alive.

Whee!

Most anemones attach themselves to a rock, a shell, or even the back of a crab. And once they find a home, they're unlikely to move, but some have been seen somersaulting across the sand!

Clownfish often make their homes in bended anemones and are sometimes called "clown anemones."

Scientific Name: Heteractis aurora
Size: Tentacles grow up to 2 inches long
Habitat: Tide pools and warmer waters
Diet: Plankton or anything else caught in their stinging tentacles

One Tough Cookie

Meet the world's scariest starfish. The knobby sea star. It's covered in black bumps that look like miniature volcanoes. They don't do much except scare away predators. But the adaptation works so well that some small animals stay safe by making their homes on the surface of the knobby starfish. Few predators dare to disturb them there. Would you want to snack on something that looks like it's about to blow up?

Scientific Name: Protoreaster nodosus
Size: Up to 12 inches across
Habitat: Tropical waters of the Pacific ocean
Diet: Coral, sponges, sea snails, urchin

Some people think the bumps on this starfish look like horns. Others say they look like chocolate chips. Or the black stripes football players paint under their eyes! What do you think they look like?

A Five-Star Water System

Starfish are perfectly adapted to life in the water. The water in their bodies gives healthy sea stars their plump shape. They move by taking in water and pumping it to the hundreds of feet that lie beneath their legs. And instead of using blood to move nutrients through their bodies, starfish use water.

Behind the Lens

Now it's your turn! Grab a camera and start shooting whenever you see something that amazes you or makes you curious to learn more. If you want to go macro without spending too much money, snap a macro lens band over a cellphone camera. Whatever camera you use, these tips will help you get started.

The flash lights the subject.

The shutter acts like a camera, opening and closing to let light into the camera for short periods of time.

The lens is the curved piece of glass that light travels through before reaching a sensor or film inside the camera.

A tripod keeps the camera steady.

The size of the opening in the lens is the aperture. It's measured in fractions.

The focal point is the part of the image that's sharp.

The depth of field is the distance between the parts of an object that are in focus. In micro and macro photography, this distance is very small.

Some lenses have a short focal length and produce a wider angle of view. Other lenses have a longer focal length.

Aperture Scale

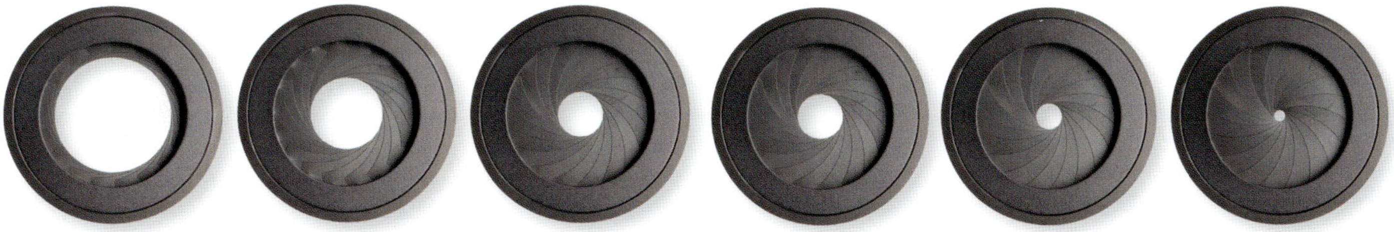

f/1.4 f/2.8 f/5.6 f/8 f/16 f/22

Large aperture ↔ Small aperture

More light strikes image sensor ↔ Less light strikes image sensor

Shallow Depth of Field (Focus) ↔ Deep Depth of Field (Focus)

Index